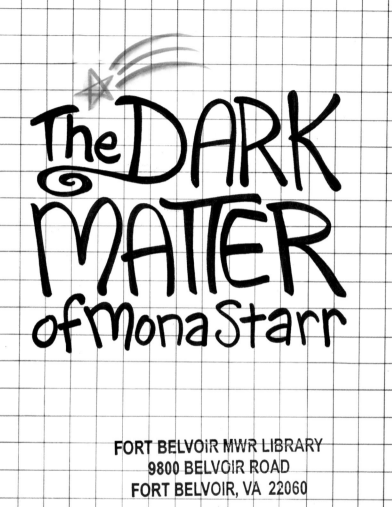

The DARK MATTER of Mona Starr

Laura Lee Gulledge

Amulet Books, New York

Library of Congress Control Number 2019945549

Hardcover ISBN 978-1-4197-3423-6
Paperback ISBN 978-1-4197-4200-2

Text and illustrations copyright © 2020 Laura Lee Gulledge
Book design by Max Temescu
Additional material by Earl Vallery (page 19), Juliet Trail (page 51), Andrea Sparacio (page 88),
and Bonnie Rubrecht (page 93). Mona's wall installation (pages 173–179) contains additional
material by Aiden, Alessa, Ally, Alyssa, And, Chaya, Christine, Cong, Daniel, Eric, Jack, Hoang,
Jaiyi, Julian, Justin, Khan, Kaiwen, Kyle, Lauren, Mai, Mia, Ruiqi, Tat, Tran, Vlassios, Will, and
Yue of Fairmont Prep Academy (Anaheim, CA), plus Anish and Abby from Skyline Middle School
(Harrisonburg, VA), plus Kiera and Makenzie from Crossroads College Preparatory School (St.
Louis, MO), plus Heidy, Salina, Makenna, Jasmine, Brandyn, and Tamia from Falling Creek
Middle School (North Chesterfield, VA), in addition to Ariana Kerr.

Published in 2020 by Amulet Books, an imprint of ABRAMS.

Printed and bound in China
10 9 8 7 6 5 4 3 2

Amulet Books are available at special discounts when purchased
in quantity for premiums and promotions as well as fundraising or
educational use. Special editions can also be created to specification.
For details, contact specialsales@abramsbooks.com
or the address below.

Amulet Books® is a registered trademark of Harry N. Abrams, Inc.

ABRAMS The Art of Books
195 Broadway, New York, NY 10007
abramsbooks.com

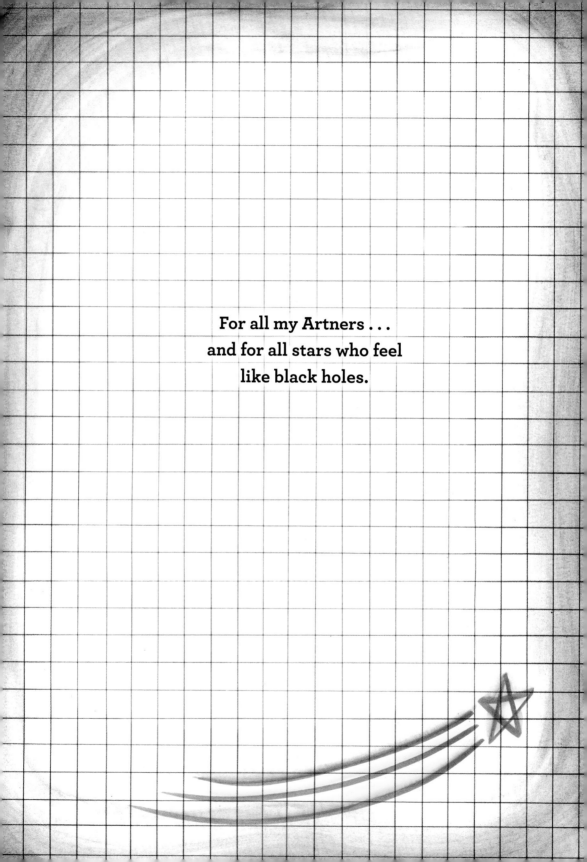

For all my Artners . . .
and for all stars who feel
like black holes.

2

Do you have any other friends you can talk to besides Nash?

Not really. I've kinda been a loner.

My childhood friends went to a different middle school, so I started over...

But then my new friends all went to a different high school.

PAT PAT

It was okay because I had Nash as my constant. My fellow weirdo.

We share a love of sci-fi, making playlists, puns, nachos, and questioning reality.

6

7

11

16

17

A - Mix CD
B - Macadamia nuts
C - Kukui nut necklace
D - Blank book
E - Plumeria hairclip
F - Pressed fern
G - Nene magnet
H - Lava rock
I - Postcard
J - Book list

24

25

30

31

Oh—am I in your spot?? I can move!

No, I, um . . . just wanted to welcome you to our school's best lunchtime hiding spot.

I'm Mona. Mona Starr. With two Rs.

. . . Hi.

My name is Hailey with a Y, not two Es. Wanna join me?

Yeah, sure!

So where are you from, Hailey?

Texas. My family just moved here. With our dozen cats.

Dozen?!

Heh, yeah, my mom is into animal rescue.

37

Gifts
can come
wrapped
in curses

42

44

51

52

Consider this—What if you BOTH need each other?

Cheesy factor reaching danger levels!!!

Seriously, Mona: don't self-sabotage on me. If you're going to give her a shot...

...then REALLY give her a shot!

Yes, sir.

55

64

68

69

71

72

Maybe
this is where
I belong.

On a scale of one to ten, what's your pain level?

When it's bad it's a... seven?

Have you felt this pain before?

No. Wait...

Yes! Six months ago! I forgot about it.

Well, we can't identify a problem. You seem healthy.

Then we need to run more tests!!

97

112

114

117

120

126

136

142

146

147

148

154

After all, if I can find a way to change my story...

...maybe I can help change some of the other stories.

Visionary
Resilient
Worthy
Connected
Lucky
Valuable

Vulnerable?

Yes, that's it! Artner Dare 2.0 requires us all to come out of our

 I think you have a solid plan! You've covered all your bases.

But what if we get into trouble? What if people are offended? What if no one participates? What if we become a meme?

 What if there is the robot uprising? RELAX, you got this.

WHO ARE YOU?? I guess you have gotten swept up in that aloha spirit…

 What's wrong with that? As a wise man once said…

"Go that way. Really fast. If something gets in your way… turn!"

 Like, sure I'm worried this volcano will erupt. But there's nothing I can do to prevent it. So why stress?

Future you will figure it out. I just wish I could be there to help.

Mahalo, Nash.

And hey, if you survive you should come visit the Big Island!

First we'll have to see how that volcano situation pans out…

Stage #3: Installation

Now we've gotta just stick to the plan. And breathe.

And hope no one takes it down before lunch!

Phew...

Acknowledgments

The support I've received to help bring this book
into the world has changed my heart forever.

First I need to thank my LITERARY ARTNERS: editors Emily Daluga
and Maggie Lehrman along with designers Siobhan Gallagher and Max
Temescu at Abrams Books, plus my literary agent Daniel Lazar at
Writers House. You wanted a story I was reluctant to tell but your
faith in Mona made be brave enough to trust where she was taking us.

Another big thanks goes to my CONTRIBUTING ARTNERS Andrea
Spracaio, Bonnie Rubrecht, Lauren Larken, Earl Vallery, and John K.
Snyder III for your incredibly helpful feedback during the editing
process. Plus extra thanks to Andrea, Bonnie, and Earl for contibuting
handwriting. And I'm extra excited to acknowledge the 37 real life
students* who gave voice to Mona's classmates in the wall installation
at the end of the book! Thanks for accepting my Artner Dare.
(*See copyright page for the full list.)

I'm especially grateful to thank all the GENEROUS PATRONS who
provided financial support which covered my housing costs during the
11 months of drawing production. This includes everyone who voted
for me to receive the local SOUP GRANT through New City Arts
Initiative in Charlottesville. Plus all the contributors to my online
PATREON CAMPAIGN: Artistic Evolution, Hina Ansari, Diana Arge
Bendixen, Bernie Beitman, Maurice and Patty Gulledge, Brian Gulledge,
Chris Grandjean, Earl Vallery, Jamie Bernstein, Jamie Linck, Jennifer
Hayden, Juliet Trail, Kenneth Hill, Lindsay Heider Diamond, Matt Mikas,
Melissa Charles, Natalie Anderson, The Moxley Family, Vivek Tiwary,
Chris Calloway, Francis Mitchell, Caitlin Adams, Ray Keilman, Alan
Reynolds, John Steimke, and Wendy Addison. It was such a
pleasure to share this journey with you all!

Special thanks go out to ARTNER ANGELS Eileen French for
welcoming me into her studio at McGuffey Arts Center while I
finished inking, my Dad for all his sanity-saving help with Photoshop,
and especially Earl for being so supportive through this emotionally
challenging process. I don't know if I could have done it without
you . . . and I will never forget all you did for Mona and I.

Finally I'd like to thank all my friends, family, Artners, students,
readers, ancestors, and animal friends who have kindly encouraged
and supported me on this long journey. This story belongs to all of us.

Thank You!

♡ artnerlove,
Laura Lee

Nash's READING LIST

1. American Nations by Colin Woodard
2. Ishmael by Daniel Quinn
3. The Fire Next Time by James Baldwin
4. The Miracle of Mindfulness by Thich Nhat Hanh
5. Women Who Run with the Wolves by Clarissa Pinkola Estés
6. Quiet: The Power of Introverts in a World that Can't Stop Talking by Susan Cain
7. Party of One: The Loner's Manifesto by Anneli Rufus
8. The Highly Sensitive Person by Elaine N. Aron
9. Lighter Than My Shadow by Katie Green
10. Marbles: Mania, Depression, Michelangelo and Me by Ellen Forney

Mona's SOUNDTRACK

1. "Ode to My Family" - The Cranberries
2. "Tomorrow, Tomorrow" - Elliott Smith
3. "Saying Goodbye" - J.S. Ondara
4. "Everybody Here Hates You" - Courtney Barnett
5. "Phenomenal Woman" - Laura Mvula
6. "Breaking Down" - Florence + the Machine
7. "Comptine D'Un Autre Été L'Après Midi" - Yann Tiersen
8. "Hospital Beds" - Cold War Kids
9. "Cosmic Girl" - Jamiroquai
10. "While My Guitar Gently Weeps" - The Beatles
11. "Without You" - Harry Nilsson
12. "Invisible Sun" - The Police
13. "Remind Me" - Emily King
14. "Turn the Light" - Karen O & Danger Mouse
15. "Invincible" - Muse
16. "Dark Matter" - Andrew Bird
17. "Bad Day" - R.E.M.
18. "Lightning Bolt" - Jake Bugg
(and the entire album A Moon Shaped Pool by Radiohead)

NOTE: I don't always do everything listed here! It's an ideal list since real life demands flexibility. But I manage to do most of it, which has vastly improved my life and helped me make smarter decisions...

Laura Lee's
Self-Care Plan
Hero's Training Regimen ↑

Physical Needs

DAILY
8 hours of sleep
Supplements & Food Medicine
No caffeine after 2 pm
Affection XO (8 hugs a day!)
Stretching breaks from desk work

WEEKLY
Walking in nature 2 hours
Yoga 1 hour
Physical Therapy 1 hour
(Adult beverages: limit 3x)
Flossing & face scrub

REGULARLY
Wear wrist brace while cleaning
Hot baths & steaming
Seasonal healing (like massage)

Daily Supplements

Wheat germ
Prunes
Kombucha
Tulsi tea
Local, fresh
  real food

Ginger turmeric shots
Multivitamin
Fish oil
Probiotic
Vitamin D
Calcium

Support System

WORLD FAMILY:
Earl
Juliet
Larken
Bonnie
Sam

BIOLOGICAL FAMILY:
Mom
Dad
Brian
Anna
Elaine

+ Artners,
Readers,
Historical
Mentors,
Ancestors,
& Magical
Helpers

When stress symptoms flare up... do some things from your self-care plan! And reach out to someone in your support system.

Emotional Needs

Time in nature
Time with animals
Time with kids
Time in water
Growing plants
Singing in studio & car
Making playlists & listening to radio
Ecstatic Dance
Prayer/devotion rituals
Exploring new places
Introvert Social recovery time
Aromatherapy/scent scene changes
Phone dates with support system
Friend dates in person
Sending snail mail
Volunteering

Mental Needs

WEEKLY
1–2 days off & flex time
Fictional assistant time
Contemplative chores
  (like washing dishes)

REGULARLY
Personal art time
Journaling
Alone time
Artnering with others
Learning new things

DAILY
Know my WARNING SIGNS
Meditate 10 min
Avoid violent content
No screens after 9:30 pm
Limited social media
Controlled news intake
Periods of silence
Reading for fun

Stress Warning Signs

Insomnia
Melancholia
Appetite loss
Overindulgence $
Working late
Racing thoughts
Racing heart
Excessive nail/cuticle biting
Feeling overwhelmed
Increased insecurity/doubt
Pain in neck, back, wrist, or belly
Hunched over posture
Excessive future tripping or nostalgia
Eye styes/twitching, avoiding eye contact
Trouble communicating or listening

✪ When in doubt, take a shower or make tea!

What helps YOU feel better? Fill out your own self-care plan and post it somewhere in your home or studio. Share it with the people in your life who care about you so they know your needs and help remind you to do the things that keep you healthy when you are struggling.

Self-Care Plan

Physical Needs

Daily Supplements

Support System

Emotional Needs

Stress Warning Signs

Mental Needs

Need more time? Make a TIME CHART of how you honestly spend your time during an average week. What can you take time away from to devote to self-care?

✪ When in doubt,

About the Author

LAURA LEE GULLEDGE is an author, illustrator, teaching artist, and proponent of Artner love.

Her debut YA graphic novel *Page by Paige* was nominated for the prestigious Eisner and Harvey Awards. Her second graphic novel *Will & Whit* was selected as a YALSA Top Ten Book for Teens and has been adapted into an innovative multidisciplinary musical. Then her interactive book *Sketchbook Dares: 24 Ways to Draw Out Your Inner Artist* invites you to try out her favorite drawing activities.

Laura Lee also enjoys exploring comics journalism, interactive event production, ecstatic dance, live art performance, and sustainable creativity. She currently lives in Charlottesville, Virginia, where she posts new art and adventures weekly in her blog at WHOISLAURALEE.COM.

*A couple examples of art imitating life: Laura Lee playing violin in high school orchestra and about to go into emergency surgery, just like Mona.

Author's Note

I used to fear that embracing my artistic side would make me more "crazy," or it would reveal there was something deeply wrong with me. But it turns out it's not the art that makes you mentally unhealthy . . . it's NOT making art. Because no matter how "normal" I acted, my overwhelming thoughts were still there eating away at me.

Thankfully, I surrendered to my creative impulses and learned to use them as a resource to help me express, understand, and heal myself. I got to know the voices in my head and how to manage them, which has saved my life in so many ways.

And miraculously, this resource is available to everyone.

If YOU have a creative outlet, no matter what medium or level of quality it may be, I encourage you to please use it. Use your gifts and resources. Pay attention to your thoughts and emotions. Find a way to get them out. Share the journey. Find your Artners. And ask for help if you need it.

. . . I ARTNER DARE YOU.

*Laura Lee's artwork from high school.